Dangerous Game

WILLIAM HARRIS

Series Editor

Library Learning Information

Idea Store® Chrisp Street
1 Vesey Path
East India Dock Road
London E14 6BT

020 7364 4332

Created and managed by
Tower Hamlets Council

Pearson Education Limited
Edinburgh Gate, Harlow,
Essex CM20 2JE, England
and Associated Companies throughout the world.

ISBN 0 582 42746 0

This edition first published 2000

3 5 7 9 10 8 6 4

NEW EDITION

Copyright © Penguin Books Ltd 2000
Illustrations by Biz Hull
Cover design by Bender Richardson White

Typeset by Bender Richardson White
Set in 11/14pt Bembo
Printed in China
SWTC/03

Published by Pearson Education Limited in association with
Penguin Books Ltd, both companies being subsidiaries of Pearson Plc

For a complete list of titles available in the Penguin Readers series, please write to your local
Pearson Education office or to: Penguin Readers Marketing Department,
Pearson Education, Edinburgh Gate, Harlow, Essex CM20 2JE.

Contents

Tower Hamlets	
Suppliers Code	AVA
Price	£4.30
Invoice Date	01/11/2006
LOC	CHR
Class	428.6
Barcode	C001277000

Introduction

My name is William Harris. I'm forty-eight years old. Perhaps you've heard of me. I'm not famous, but many people have heard of me. You see, I'm a writer. I've written about twenty-five books. I write all kinds of stories: love stories, detective stories and – yes, ghost stories. But don't get the wrong idea. This isn't just another ghost story. This is different from any story that I've ever written. Why? Because it's a true story. Everything in this story has really happened . . .

For a number of years, William Harris plays a game with a ghost before he goes to sleep. The ghost is a poltergeist that William calls 'Poldy'. At the beginning William and Poldy play a friendly game every night, but then the game begins to go wrong. It becomes a dangerous game: the *Dangerous Game* that gives this story its title.

Louis Alexander was born in London in 1932. He completed his studies at London University in 1954 and then taught English as a Foreign Language in a number of countries.

He is best known as the writer of English language courses like *New Concept English* (1967), *Look Listen and Learn* (1971), *Follow Me* (1980) and *Direct English* (1993-1998); practice books like *For and Against* (1968); grammars like the *Longman English Grammar* (1988), and readers like *K's First Case* (also a Penguin Reader).

He and his wife Julia live in London.

Chapter 1   I'll Begin at the Beginning

I don't know when the game began.

My wife died twelve years ago and the game began soon after that. But I can't remember exactly when. I continued to live in this house after she died. I still live here. It's a big house, but I don't want to move to a smaller place. I love this house and everything in it. You see, I haven't got many friends, and all the things in this house are important to me. I can't live without them.

Some time after my wife's death, I realized that my bedroom was haunted. It's the only room in the house that's haunted. One night, I suddenly realized there was a ghost in the room. I wasn't afraid because this ghost was friendly. It was a happy ghost. I always wanted to laugh when it was in the room. You'll say it was my wife's ghost. I don't know. I always think of the ghost as 'he', not 'she'. I named the ghost 'Poldy'. I made up the name 'Poldy' from the word 'poltergeist'. You know that a poltergeist is a playful ghost. It likes to drop things on the floor; it likes to make a noise; it likes to throw things round the room. It likes to move your bed and to play games. Poldy was friendly and playful, so we made up a little game. We play it every night. We've played it for years now. In fact, I must *always* play the game before I go to sleep. I can't go to sleep if I don't play it. Poldy doesn't 'appear' at midnight or anything like that. He's not that kind of ghost. He's always in the room. But he only appears when we play the game. Of course, I don't *have* to play the game, but I always *want* to play. I know Poldy does too. I'm writing this story because I want to tell you about this game. Nobody knows about it. My best friend (perhaps he's my only friend) doesn't know about it. I know about it and Poldy knows about it, and that's all. It's our secret. But I'm talking too much. When you live alone, you're always talking to yourself! I must begin at the beginning.

My name is William Harris. I'm forty-eight years old. Perhaps you've heard of me. I'm not famous, but many people have heard of me. You see, I'm a writer. I've written about twenty-five books. I write all kinds of stories: love stories, detective stories and – yes, ghost stories. But don't get the wrong idea. This isn't just another ghost story. This is different from any story that I've ever written. Why? Because it's a *true* story. Everything in this story has really happened. In fact, strange things are still happening.

I'm not a famous writer, but my books sell quite well. I have the money to live in this nice house. I can live in the way that I want to live. I'm not rich, but I'm not poor, either. I live simply. I've always lived simply. When my wife was alive, I didn't live very simply. We went out a lot. We had a lot of friends. Since she died, I don't go out very much. I like to stay at home and write my books. (Just now, I'm writing another detective story. My readers like my detective stories best. I made up the famous detective Filbert Wiley. Perhaps you've heard of him. Perhaps you've read one of my Filbert Wiley stories.) I've stopped work on my new Filbert Wiley book to write this story. I have to write it now while there's still time.

But I must tell you something about myself first, and about my wife. Ah! Life was very different for me when she was alive. My wife's name was Julie. She was two years younger than I was. She was completely different from me. She liked to dance and sing; she liked to go to parties. Our house was always full of people in those days. 'Put a suit on, William!' she often said to me. (I don't like suits.) 'Put a suit on' meant many things. Perhaps we were going out. Perhaps friends were coming to dinner. Perhaps we were having a party. I could never be sure. Anything could happen. I never knew about it before it happened. My life was in Julie's hands. Without her I was nothing. I didn't want to meet the world, so Julie brought the world to me.

It was a wonderful life! It was wonderful because Julie made it like that. All our friends were jealous of me. 'Lucky old William!' they often said. 'Lucky man to have a wife like that! He's so quiet and so uninteresting, and she's so alive!' Oh yes, they were jealous. You don't often see happy people, *really* happy people, I mean. And we were happy. That was our secret. Love was our secret. I loved Julie and she loved me. Then, suddenly, Julie became ill, very ill. I called the best doctors, but they couldn't do anything. I looked after her day and night. But in two short months she was dead. Dead! I couldn't believe it. I still can't believe it after all these years. When she died, part of me died with her. Now she lives in my memory. I can't forget her and will never forget her. I didn't want to look for another wife. Julie was my wife for twelve years and now she's been dead for twelve years. Sadly, we never had any children. So when she died, I was alone. I shut myself in my house. I did nothing except work. At first, I wrote my books because I didn't want to think of my dear wife. The pain was too great. In time things were a little better, but the pain has never really gone. I still feel it sharply when I think of Julie. She's still alive in my memory.

Of course, I lost nearly all my friends – all those jealous friends. They liked Julie, but they didn't like me very much. Without Julie, I didn't go out. I didn't go to parties. I didn't ask other people to come to my house and all my 'friends' soon left me. Nobody was jealous of me. I wasn't 'lucky old William'; just 'poor old William'. Now I have only one real friend. His name is

Louis. He's a writer too. But I don't know anything about his books. I haven't read any of them. In fact, I haven't seen his books in any bookshop. Louis and I never talk about books. That's because we have the same interests. We both like chess. We have a game of chess once a week. Louis comes to see me every Wednesday. He always arrives at eight o'clock in the evening and we play chess for about three hours. Sometimes we play a number of games; sometimes only one. At about eleven, Louis goes home and I go to bed and play a different kind of game with Poldy, but I'll tell you about that later. Louis is really a very good friend. We play chess and never talk very much. Sometimes we don't say anything all evening. Good friends don't need to talk. Louis knows me very well and I know him very well. We've been friends since we were students together. Louis was my friend before I met Julie. He knows a lot about me. But there are some things that he doesn't know. He'll be surprised when he reads this story.

Louis and I have played chess together for years. He often came here when Julie was alive. Julie and I never went to parties on a Wednesday, because that was always my day. I must tell you that Louis will be here tomorrow. It's Tuesday today. Tuesday morning. I'm sitting at my desk in my study. I'm writing this story. The winter sun is shining through my study window. It's a beautiful day, but I don't want to go out. I never want to go out these days. Filbert Wiley is my only company. Just now I'm very tired: very, very sleepy because I didn't sleep well last night. I played a game with Poldy and it didn't end for a very long time. I'll tell you about this game, but not yet.

Well, that's my life. It's a very simple life and not a very interesting one, is it? How can life without Julie be interesting? Here I am, a middle-aged writer, alone in a big house. I have only one real friend in the world. I have my books. I have Filbert Wiley, the famous detective. Perhaps I live through Filbert. I have my chess and I have my memories. But it's not a sad life and it's not a very quiet life. A lot happens in this house. There's a lot of noise and laughter . . . because I have Poldy. And I haven't told you anything about Poldy – yet! Poldy and laughter go together. I mean, they went together at first!

I don't know when the game began. I've already told you that. I can't remember when I first met Poldy. But I can remember very clearly *how* I met him. I can remember the first time that he 'appeared'. The first time that I realized he was in my bedroom. I can remember every detail. So I want to tell you about it in detail. My bedroom wasn't haunted when Julie was alive. Or perhaps it was and I didn't realize it. I'll never know.

Do you believe in ghosts? I've written a number of ghost stories, but they were only stories. I never believed in ghosts before. And I'm not sure I do now. But I know one thing. I'm sure there's a poltergeist in my bedroom. I can't say more than that.

Here are a few details about my bedroom. You need to know them before I can tell my story. There's a big double bed in the room. Yes, it's the same double bed that Julie and I slept in. The head of the bed is against a wall. I sleep on one side of the bed. It's the same side that I've always slept on. There's a bedside table next to the bed. There's a bedside light on the table. There's a light socket near the floor. The light socket is for my bedside light. My light has a long cord. There's a plug at the end of the cord and this plug goes into the light socket. Don't laugh at these details. They're all very important. You'll understand the reason soon.

One dark winter night, I was reading in bed. It wasn't an interesting book and I was very sleepy. I usually switch off the light when I want to go to sleep. (My light has a small white switch.) But that night I didn't switch off the light in the usual way. (I don't know why.) Strangely, I reached over the side of the bed and pulled the plug out of the socket. Why did I do this? I still don't know. It was a funny thing to do. When I pulled the plug out, I suddenly wasn't sleepy. I was awake – really awake. The room was dark, completely black, but my eyes were wide open. My book fell to the floor. It hit the floor with a loud sound, but I didn't notice. I sat up in bed with my eyes open. I rested my back against the head of the bed. I looked into the dark room. Of course, I couldn't see anything. But just then, I knew there was someone in the room. I didn't know *where* in the room, but it? he? she? was somewhere in front of me. Many minutes passed. I looked hard into the dark. I waited, but I still couldn't see anything. I wasn't afraid. The 'person' in the room was very friendly. I was happy. I couldn't hear anything, but there was laughter in the air. 'Who is it?' I called. 'Who's there?' But there was no answer. I waited for a long time. The 'person' in the room was a friend, a good friend. I wanted to meet this friend very much. 'If I switch on the light, perhaps I'll see him,' I thought. I pressed the switch on my bedside light. I pressed it on and off, but nothing happened. Then I remembered. The plug wasn't in its socket! So I reached over the side of the bed and pushed the plug back into the socket. Suddenly, the light came on. The room was empty. I could feel it. I knew the 'person' wasn't there. I pulled the plug out again and waited. Nothing. The room was still empty. I put the plug in and the light came on again. There was still nobody there. I switched the light off (from the light switch), but nothing happened. I was alone without my friend. I stayed awake for many hours. I thought, 'It's a poltergeist,' and immediately the name 'Poldy' came into my head. I called out, 'Poldy! Poldy!' but he didn't come back. In the end I fell asleep. But I knew something important was happening to me. This was my first meeting with the friendly ghost, my first meeting with Poldy. This was the beginning.

Chapter 2 The Game

I woke up late the next morning.

The cold winter sun was already up. My room was light. I sat up in bed and thought about the night before. Did those things really happen? Was it all a dream? I looked over the side of the bed. Yes, my book was on the floor. I looked at the light and the plug. Yes, the plug was in its socket. The details were right. I got up slowly. I washed and had breakfast. Then I went to my study. (I was writing a detective story at the time, I remember.) The adventures of Filbert Wiley soon filled my day and I forgot about the adventures of the night before.

I finished work early. I wasn't sleepy in the evening, but I went to bed earlier than usual – at about ten o'clock. I sat in bed and thought about the night before. I didn't want to read, so I sat quietly with the light on. Then, very carefully, I switched it off (from the light switch) and waited. I looked into the dark room. Nothing happened. The room was 'empty'. 'This is silly,' I thought. I switched the light on again and got a book – an interesting one this time. I read for a long time and began to feel sleepy. I put my book on the bedside table. Then I wanted to switch the light off. But I didn't use the switch – I don't know why. Strangely, I reached over the side of the bed and found the cord. Then I found the plug and pulled it out of the socket. Immediately, I knew Poldy was there. The friendly ghost was somewhere in the room. 'Poldy!' I called. There was no answer. I

got out of bed and walked round the room. Poldy was there. I knew it. In the end, I went back to bed. I reached over the side and pushed the plug into its socket. The light came on. Poldy wasn't there. When I switched the light off again (from the switch) he didn't come back. I switched the light on and off a number of times, but nothing happened. So I went to sleep.

The next night I made an important discovery. It was my first important discovery: the first of a number of discoveries. I went to bed at my usual time. I didn't read. I immediately switched off the light (from the light switch) and waited for Poldy, but he didn't 'appear'. But when I pulled the plug out of the socket, he 'appeared'. Or I felt he was there. When I put the plug back in, he 'disappeared'. This was my important discovery. Poldy *never* 'appeared' when I used the light switch. He appeared *only* when I pulled the plug out. He appeared only once. When I put the plug back in, he disappeared. He didn't come back.

I tried this the night after. I pulled the plug out when I went to bed. Poldy was there. I put it back and the light came on: Poldy wasn't there. I pulled the plug out again, but he didn't come back. After that I put it back and pulled it out a number of times, but nothing happened. So I knew. Poldy came only *once*: when I pulled the plug out. He went away when I put it back.

For many nights after that, I enjoyed Poldy's company. Sometimes I sat in the dark for hours with Poldy in the room. I enjoyed this very much. I could 'bring' him into the room or I could 'send him away' with the light plug, but I could only do it once. I could keep the plug out of its socket for a long time. In that way I was able to enjoy Poldy's company for hours and hours. I was *happy* when Poldy was in the room. I often called to him, but he never gave me any sign of his presence. I could only 'feel' his presence: there was no other sign.

I never told anyone about Poldy. Louis came on Wednesdays and we played chess, but I never told him my secret. One

Wednesday evening he said to me: 'You're very well, William. Always smiling and happy. It's nice to see you like this. Perhaps you have a secret life!' I smiled and said nothing. It was true of course: I had a secret life, but I didn't tell Louis about it. I know he's my best, my only friend. But I don't think he can understand things like this.

I enjoyed Poldy's company in this way for nearly a year. Then one night something strange happened. I pulled the plug out and Poldy was in my room. I was sitting in bed. I called out to him: 'Poldy!' and he gave me the first sign of his presence. I heard a knock. It came from the other side of the room. Then there was another knock. The knocks got louder and came nearer and nearer to my bed. Then the knocking stopped. I wasn't afraid: in fact, I laughed. Then the knocking began again: it moved away from my bed to the other side of the room. It was a strange knocking sound. How can I describe it? Well, it was like someone with a wooden leg. It was like a wooden leg on the floor. When a man walks with a wooden leg, you can hear a knock. Knock, knock, knock – like that. I was very happy. At last I had a sign from Poldy. I could feel he was there. And I could hear he was there. 'He's not afraid of me,' I thought. 'So he's given me a sign.'

Every day I worked in my usual way, but my life was different now. Every night I enjoyed Poldy's company. He became more and more friendly. He gave me different signs of his presence. Sometimes he shook my bed. I laughed and he shook it again. Or sometimes he shook a chair in my room. I could hear it on the floor. Or sometimes he threw things round the room. I couldn't see them in the dark, but I could hear them. Once a hand-mirror flew right past my face. Sometimes Poldy opened and shut my bedroom door. He did this very quickly a number of times. Sometimes he played little jokes. Once I found my shirt in my bed. Another time I found one of my shoes in my bed. I always laughed at these jokes. I think Poldy liked to hear laughter. He always knocked at the window or shook my bed.

I tried hard to see him. I looked into the dark room, but I never saw anything. But I could feel his presence and I could hear him.

When I got tired of all these jokes, I pushed the plug back into its socket. The light came on and Poldy went away. Then I always switched the light off and went to sleep.

One night I made my second important discovery. Poldy was in my room. He 'walked' to my bed and away from it many times. He shook my bed and knocked at my door. In the end, I was very sleepy. 'I'll put the plug back in,' I thought. 'The light will come on and Poldy will go away. Then I'll turn it off and go to sleep.' I reached over the side of the bed and picked up the plug. Suddenly, Poldy pulled the cord and the plug flew out of my hand. I had to find it (and it wasn't easy) and I put it in the socket. But this was an important discovery. Poldy didn't just want to give me signs of his presence. He didn't just want to play little jokes. He wanted to play a game with me.

In the end, we made up this game with the light plug. The rules of the game were very simple. But it took us a long time to make them up. The rules 'grew'. They were like this:

Rule 1: I went to bed with the light still on.
Rule 2: I pulled out the plug from the socket and Poldy appeared. I didn't only feel his presence: he always gave me a clear sign. I heard 'knock, knock' at the other side of the room.
Rule 3: Poldy then began to 'walk' towards my bed. I had to put the plug back in the socket before he reached my bed. Poldy had to reach my bed before I put the plug back in. That was the game. If Poldy reached my bed first, he 'won'. He shook my bed and the game began

again. If I put the plug in first, I won. Poldy disappeared when the light came on. He didn't return.

We played this game every night for a long time, perhaps two years. Poldy usually won a number of times each night. I laughed a lot when we played. It was a very happy game. And then something went wrong. I don't know what and I don't know how. But something went wrong, very wrong.

Chapter 3 A Game of Chess

'Your move,' Louis said.

'My move?' I answered. 'I've just moved.'

'No,' Louis said. '*I've* just moved. It's your move.' He pointed at the chess board.

'Don't be silly, Louis!' I said sharply. 'I know when I've moved. And I know when I haven't moved.'

'Well, you haven't moved and it's your move,' Louis repeated. 'You aren't watching the game, William.'

'The game?' I cried suddenly. 'Which game? Who told you about the game? What do you know about the game? I've never told anyone about the game. It's my secret. Do you understand? It's my secret. Just Poldy and I . . . We . . .' I was shouting. I could hear my voice. I stopped suddenly. Louis was looking at me strangely.

'Is there anything that you want to tell me, William?'

'Eh? What?'

'Is there anything that you want to tell me? There's something on your mind.'

'There isn't anything on my mind,' I said, thinking, 'I must be more careful.' I looked up at Louis. 'You're right,' I said. 'There *is* something on my mind. It's this new Filbert Wiley story. It's on my mind all the time. It's a story about a game. The game's on my mind. I'm sorry I spoke like that a minute ago.'

'That's all right,' Louis said kindly. 'Your story sounds very interesting, but now we're playing a game of chess.'

'Yes, I must think about that,' I said.

14

'Who is this . . . this Poldy?' Louis asked.

'Poldy?' I cried. 'What do you know about Poldy? Who told you about Poldy?' I could hear my angry voice again. I was shouting. Again, I stopped suddenly. 'I'm sorry,' I said.

'*You* told me about Poldy, William,' Louis said. 'A minute ago you said: "Just Poldy and I . . . We . . ."'

'Did I say that?' I asked.

'Yes,' Louis said. 'I know you very well, William. You haven't got many friends. Is this Poldy a new friend? Poldy is a very unusual name, isn't it?'

'It *is* an unusual name,' I said. 'I'll tell you about Poldy if you want to hear about him. Poldy is only a character in my new Filbert Wiley story.'

'What sort of character?'

'I don't know. He's a playful character. He plays all kinds of jokes.'

'I mean, is he good or bad?' Louis asked.

'Oh, he's good,' I said immediately. 'A very . . . very nice – er – person. He's kind and funny and I like him a lot, but . . . but . . .'

'Yes?'

'Well, sometimes I think he's bad too. Poldy's character isn't clear in my mind. Sometimes I think he's evil. You know, *very* evil.'

'Evil? But you said he's funny and kind and playful.'

'That's an interesting point,' I said. 'Tell me, Louis. Can a person be evil and funny and kind and playful at the same time? What do you think?'

'I've never thought about it,' Louis said.

'I'll tell you about Poldy, if I can,' I said. 'I'll try to tell you. Poldy . . .'

Suddenly, I heard a loud 'knock, knock' from upstairs.

Louis and I were in the living room. The living room is below my bedroom. The 'knock, knock' came from my bedroom.

'What's the matter, William?' Louis asked. 'Your face is white. You were telling me about Poldy.'

'Did you hear a knock, Louis?' I asked. 'Like this.' I picked up a wooden chess piece and knocked on the table. 'Like a wooden leg on the floor. Like a man with a wooden leg.'

'No, of course not,' Louis said. 'I didn't hear anything.'

'But it came from upstairs.'

'No. It's very quiet in here.'

'Then I probably imagined it.'

'Yes,' Louis answered. 'You imagined it. You're a writer, William, and you live in your imagination. But you must be careful. Imagination can be dangerous.'

'In what way dangerous?'

'Well, it can rule your life. You're working too hard. You don't go out enough. You have an uninteresting life – in the real world, I mean. You're in your study all day. You're alone in this big house. Then at night you sleep and the next day you're in your study again. You need friends. You need the air and the sky and the sun. You don't live as a person but only through your imagination. And that's dangerous because adventures in the mind can rule your life. You start to think this Poldy is a real person. But he's only a character in one of your stories. He's just like Filbert Wiley. He isn't real. He doesn't exist.'

'Oh, but he *does* exist.'

'Yes, but only in your mind.'

'So he exists and is real. Hamlet was one of Shakespeare's characters. But he *exists*. He's real. Queen Elizabeth I existed. She was alive and she ruled England, but she's not *more real* than Hamlet. Don't you think that Hamlet is a real person? Like Queen Elizabeth was a real person? I mean they're both real persons in our minds.'

'That's an interesting point,' Louis said. 'Things can exist in the mind or in the real world. So the character in your story – this Poldy – is "real" to you. And I'm "real" to you in the same way. Right?'

'Right,' I said.

'I always knew you were a thinker, William,' Louis said. 'Now let's get back to this game of chess. It's your move.'

'*My* move? I've just moved.'

'Let's not start that again. Look, we'll go through the moves from the beginning. I'm white and you're black. Right?'

'Right.'

Louis went through the game from the beginning.

'We've both moved fourteen times,' Louis said. 'I'm white so I moved first. Now I've just moved again: that's the fifteenth move. And it's your move.'

I looked at the chess board hard for a long time. 'You're right,' I said. 'I wasn't watching the game.'

'Yes, I told you that,' Louis answered. 'Your mind's on other things.'

'Well, I'm looking at the game now and I don't like it. It's gone wrong.'

'Not for me, but for you,' Louis said.

'Yes,' I answered. 'Something's wrong, very wrong. I can't do anything about it.' I moved my king.

Louis immediately moved his queen. He picked up the big wooden chess piece and put it down hard on the chess board. It hit the board with a loud knock.

'You can't move anywhere,' Louis said loudly. 'I'm afraid you've lost the game.'

I looked at the chess board. 'You're right,' I said. 'I can't move the king anywhere.'

'You didn't play very well,' Louis said. 'You didn't play your usual game.'

'I know,' I answered.

'Do you know why?' Louis asked.

'No. Why? Tell me.'

'Because your mind wasn't on the game. Your mind was on this character, Poldy. *I* didn't win. Poldy won.'

'How?'

'Because he rules your mind. Thinkers and writers must live too. Their ideas mustn't rule their lives.'

'You're right, Louis,' I said.

Louis looked at his watch. 'Mmm,' he said. 'It's ten to twelve. It's late. I must go.' He got up. 'Thanks for the game, William. Good night and I'll see you next week.'

'Thank you, Louis,' I said. 'Good night.' I got up and suddenly knocked the chess board off the table. It hit the floor and the pieces went across the room.

'You've really lost the game now,' Louis laughed.

Chapter 4   The Game Goes Wrong

That game of chess was about five years ago.

Of course, I've played chess with Louis once a week since then. I'll have a game with him tomorrow. But I've described that game of chess because I remember it in detail. At that time my game with Poldy was beginning to go wrong. This didn't happen suddenly. Oh, no. It happened slowly, very slowly. I didn't really notice it at first.

Louis never spoke to me about Poldy again and of course I never spoke about Poldy. Louis believed that Poldy was a character in my detective story. He doesn't know that Poldy *really* exists. Poldy doesn't exist only in my mind or in my imagination, but he exists in the real world. He lives in my room. Sometimes I don't think of it as *my* room, but as Poldy's room.

I nearly forgot to be careful that night with Louis. I talked about Poldy and that was wrong. I know that Poldy heard me. The loud 'knock, knock' from upstairs was a message. Of course, Louis didn't hear it because it was a message for me. Poldy was saying, 'Be quiet, William! This is our secret, remember?' So I've been very careful since then. I never speak about my work because I don't want Louis to ask any questions about Poldy.

Things began to go wrong and this happened little by little. I first noticed it about two months before the game of chess with Louis. One night Poldy and I were playing our usual game. I pulled the plug out of its socket and the room was dark. I always 'feel' that Poldy is there. After that, he gives me a clear sign of his presence. Sometimes he knocks on the floor, sometimes on the window. Sometimes he shakes my bed. But that night Poldy didn't give me a sign. I felt he was there. That was all. I sat up in bed and called to him. 'Poldy! You're there, I know. I'm ready to play. Are you ready?'

But nothing happened.

I got out of bed and walked round the room. I walked very quietly across the wooden floor. My footsteps were very light, but I could hear them. Suddenly, I thought Poldy was behind me. I stopped and turned round. Of course, I didn't see anything. I walked up and down the room and stopped suddenly a number of times. Poldy was following me. I stood and listened. Then I heard a soft knock on the floor. It was right behind me. It got louder and louder. I turned round and it stopped.

I was angry. 'What are you doing, Poldy?' I asked. 'You're not playing the game. Are you going to play the game or aren't you? Very well,' I said. 'I'm going to punish you. I'm going back to bed. I'm going to put the plug in and send you away. I'm going to punish you.'

I climbed back into bed. 'I'll try again,' I said. 'Do you want to play or not?' Again, nothing happened. 'I'll count up to three,' I said. I counted slowly. 'One. Two. Three.' I reached over the side of the bed and touched the floor with my hand. I found the cord, but suddenly the cord began to move through my hand. I held it and pulled, but Poldy pulled too. I pulled with one hand and I tried to find the plug with the other. I was nearly on the floor now. I found the plug and pushed it in. The light came on and Poldy wasn't there.

I switched off the light from the switch, but lay awake for a long time. My heart was going wildly. 'That's funny,' I thought. 'Why doesn't he play? He's like a little boy. Perhaps he wants to change the rules. He's playing jokes.' But in my heart I knew Poldy wasn't playing jokes. I then made my third important discovery. Something was wrong with our game. After that, it was never the same again.

The next night I was afraid. This was the first time that I felt fear in my games with Poldy. I couldn't pull the plug out. I lay in bed for a long time with the light on. I was really afraid. At last I was ready. 'What's going to happen,' I thought, 'when I pull the plug out?'

But Poldy didn't play any jokes. We played our usual happy game. I enjoyed it and Poldy enjoyed it.

For many nights after that, we played our game. 'Well, perhaps I've made a mistake,' I thought. 'Nothing has changed. Poldy was only playing jokes that night.'

But I was wrong.

I had a very bad night before my game of chess with Louis (the game that I've already described). There was a full moon that night, so I didn't close the curtains. I always closed the curtains, but not this time. The room was full of light. My light was on when I got into bed. After a short time, I pulled the plug out. I was ready to begin the game. But nothing happened. Poldy gave no sign. He was there, of course. I sat in bed and waited. I could see the full moon through my window. There were dark shadows on the floor. There were shadows on the walls. I could hear a cat outside. It was crying like a baby. I don't like that noise. I got up and opened the window. 'Ssshh!' I cried. The cat stopped. Then it started again. 'Ssshh!' I cried again. I saw the cat: a fat black one. It ran across the garden. 'Good,' I thought. I went back to bed. 'Are we going to play or aren't we?' I asked. I could see the room clearly. I could see the chair with my clothes on it. I could see the big wardrobe in the corner of the room. I looked at the wardrobe. I looked at it for a long time. Suddenly, the wardrobe door began to open very quietly. Just a little at first. Then more and more. Soon it was wide open.

I keep my clothes in the wardrobe. I haven't got many clothes because I don't need them. There are a few shirts, two pairs of trousers, two suits and an old coat.

The wardrobe door was wide open, so I could see inside. I saw my shirts, my suits and the coat. Then my coat began to move. It 'stepped' outside the wardrobe. It stood in front of the wardrobe door.

'Poldy,' I said slowly.

Poldy (or the coat) didn't listen to me. It stood there like a person: a person without a head or legs or hands. Then it began to 'walk' towards me. After a few slow steps, it put up an 'arm' and shook it at me.

I was angry with Poldy. 'I've had enough of your silly jokes!' I cried. 'I'm going to punish you. I'm going to send you away. If you won't play, then I must punish you.' I reached over the side of the bed and picked up the plug. It was easy to find in the moonlight. 'See?' I asked and held up the plug. 'I'm going to put it in the socket now and you're going to go away.'

The coat moved suddenly towards me. An arm reached for the plug and took it from my hands. The cord went through my fingers and the light fell onto the floor.

I got up angrily. The coat dropped the plug and went back into the wardrobe quickly. The wardrobe door shut with a loud noise. I picked up the light and put it back onto the bedside table. Then I went towards the wardrobe. I opened it a little. I put my hand inside and felt the clothes. My coat was in its place. I could feel it. It was soft and empty. I pulled the wardrobe door open and looked inside. It was empty, quite empty: there was no sign of Poldy.

'I see,' I said. 'You want me to close the curtains before we play.' I went to the window and looked out. The black cat was there again. It was still crying like a baby. 'Ssshh!' I shouted, but it didn't stop. I put my hand on the curtain, and then I noticed something. Someone was standing behind the curtain. I could clearly see the

shape of a 'person' behind the curtain. I tried to close it, but I couldn't. The 'person' didn't let me. 'Oh!' I shouted angrily. 'This is stupid!' I went back to bed and the curtain moved across the window. Now the room was in complete darkness. 'So you want to play now,' I said. There was no answer, of course – just the sound of the cat outside the window. I reached for the plug on the floor, found it and put it in the socket. The light came on. Poldy wasn't there.

Again, I lay awake for a long time. 'That was a bad game,' I thought, 'a very bad game.' While I lay there, I could hear my heart. It was going wildly. And I could hear the cat outside. It never stopped. It cried like a baby all night.

Chapter 5　Good Games and Bad Games

In the past five years, until the present time, I've continued to play games with Poldy. We've played every night. We've played good games and bad games. I've already described the good games. They're very simple and always fun. I'm happy when I'm playing good games. But I'm sad when I'm playing bad ones.

In what way is a 'good' game different from a 'bad' game, you will ask. Well, I've already described a few bad games. Perhaps you've noticed that in a bad game there are no rules. Anything can happen. And another thing: when I'm playing a good game, I'm never afraid. But when I'm playing a bad game, my heart is full of fear. The bad games are like an evil message.

I want to describe some of the games in the past five years. At the beginning (at the time of that game of chess with Louis) we didn't play many bad games. But after a time we played a good game one night and a bad game the next night. This was true until two years ago. And this is when I began to worry. Worry and fear were always present in my life.

Why did Poldy begin to play bad games? I've often asked myself this question and I've never been able to explain why. I've thought of many different reasons. Perhaps you can think of a few reasons. But it isn't easy to be sure.

At first I thought Poldy was jealous. Perhaps he was jealous when I won a game. So I decided to lose for a time. But he still wanted to play bad games.

Perhaps Poldy wanted to punish me. Why did he want to do that? I thought about this a lot. Perhaps Poldy was angry because I told Louis about him. But I didn't tell Louis anything. Louis thinks Poldy is a character in one of my detective stories. He doesn't know he's a ghost, a poltergeist. And the bad games began a long time *before* I said anything to Louis.

Who *is* Poldy? I've often thought about this, too. If I learn the answer to this question, perhaps I'll have the answer to my first question: Why does he want to play bad games? But I can't find the answer. I've often asked myself: 'Is Poldy the ghost of my dead wife? Is 'Poldy' really 'Julie'?' I think the answer to this question is: No. Poldy has never given me any sign. For example, there's a photo of Julie on my bedroom wall. Poldy has never shaken it or moved it. I've kept one of Julie's dresses. It's a beautiful party dress. It's in my wardrobe. Poldy has never 'touched' it. He's often taken my clothes out of the wardrobe. If Poldy is Julie, he – or she – can easily give me a sign. Julie loved me and I loved her. So I don't think Poldy is Julie. But I'm not really sure.

Is Poldy just part of my imagination? No, a thousand times no. Why? Because all these things really happen. I don't imagine them. They are *facts*. Poldy *exists*.

Little by little, Poldy and I played more and more bad games. Then I began to worry. I only wanted to play good games. How could I escape bad ones? I tried to escape them in a number of ways. I'll describe some of these ways to you.

I always know when we're going to play a bad game. I can feel evil in the air before the game begins. Then there's one thing that I always try to do. I try to pull the plug out and put it back immediately. In this way, Poldy doesn't have time to play. He goes away when the plug goes back in. Poldy was surprised when I first did this. It worked very well. But now he stops me. He knows when I'm going to try.

Here's another way I've tried to escape bad games. Remember,

Poldy only haunts my bedroom. He never haunts another part of the house. I've tried to sleep in other rooms in my house. But I can't escape a bad game like that. One night I slept in my study. I had a strange dream. I dreamt that I was sleeping in my study. In my dream, I got up and went to my bedroom. I sat in my own bed and read a book with the light on. In my dream, I pulled the plug out – and then, suddenly, I woke up. I wasn't in my study when I woke up, but in my bedroom. I was reaching over the side of the bed. The plug was in my hand. I walked to my bedroom in my sleep. Poldy did this: he pulled me back to the bedroom through my dream.

I tried another thing. I tried *not* to play the game. One night I sat in bed with the light on. Then I turned the light off from the switch. Of course (this is always the rule), Poldy didn't appear. I went to sleep easily. But during the night I suddenly woke up and switched on the light. I don't know why. I had to. Then I pulled the plug out and the game began. This happened a number of times.

You will ask me: Why don't you sell your house and go away? I've asked myself this question too. The fact is, I can't. I've often thought about it, but I can't do it. I've tried another thing. I've left my house at night and gone to a hotel. But when I do this, I can't sleep. I always leave the hotel during the night. I pay the bill at three or four o'clock in the morning and go home. It isn't easy to leave a hotel at four in the morning! (Try it and see!) After that, I go to bed and play a game with Poldy. So, you see, I can never escape a game. Poldy always finds a way to bring me back to my bedroom.

Until a year ago, we often played a lot of bad games. But Poldy never 'touched' me at any time. I often tried to 'touch' him. But he never 'touched' me. This was a kind of rule. I can't describe my fear when Poldy first 'touched' me.

It all happened one night about a year ago. I went to bed at eleven o'clock. I knew it was going to be a 'bad' night and not a 'good' night. I could feel it. I read for hours because I didn't want to pull the plug out. In the end, I was very sleepy, but of course I couldn't sleep. I reached over the side of the bed in my usual way and pulled the plug out. Immediately my eyes were wide open and I was awake. Poldy was there and we were ready for the game. During a bad game, Poldy doesn't always give a clear sign of his presence, but that night he gave a very clear sign. I lay in bed in fear and waited. Nothing happened for a minute and then the bed began to move. Poldy wasn't shaking the bed. He was lifting it off the floor! The bed moved into the air. I reached over the side and tried to touch the floor. I tried to find the plug. But I couldn't reach the floor. The bed was (I think) about a metre above the floor! Then the bed began to turn round: slowly at first. It went round and round and round, first slowly, then faster and faster and faster and faster! Suddenly, it stopped in the air and dropped to the floor quickly. It touched the floor lightly and was in its usual place: the head of the bed was against the wall, with the bedside table next to me. I tried to reach the plug. I touched the floor with my fingers and found it. I tried to put it back and then Poldy hit my hand sharply! I dropped the plug in fear. For the first time, he touched me – and he hit me!

I lay back in bed. The room was quiet. The bed didn't move. Then I felt something above my head. It was like a bird. I put my hand above my head. There was nothing there. Then something touched my hair lightly – like a soft hand. Fingers went lightly through my hair!

I jumped out of bed and ran to the other side of the room. I heard footsteps behind me. I turned round. Poldy was behind me. I turned round again and again, but Poldy was always behind me. Then he hit me in the face!

Then he began to push me. He gave me a little push at first: he pushed my face softly. After that, he began to push my arms and legs very hard. I kicked and shouted, but I couldn't stop him. I jumped back into bed and you will never believe it – Poldy bit my face very hard! I cried out in pain. I reached over the side of the bed and touched the floor. I touched it wildly to find the plug. At last, the plug was in my hand. I tried to find the socket. I touched the wall with my fingers, but in my fear I couldn't find it. 'Please! Please!' I shouted. 'Where is it? Where's the socket?' Someone or something tried to pull the plug out of my hand. But in my fear I was strong – stronger than Poldy. I pushed the plug in hard. The light came on – and suddenly, I was alone. 'Ah!' I cried. My heart went wildly and my body shook in fear.

That was a very bad night. It was the first time that Poldy ever touched me. After that, he often touched me. Sometimes he touched softly with his fingers, sometimes he pushed me, hit me or kicked me. It wasn't just a bad game now. It was a dangerous game.

We began to play more and more bad games. I've already told you that. But the number of bad games and good games was the same. That was true a year ago. But after Poldy touched me the first time, something changed. We never played another good game. During the past year we've played only bad games every night. All our games are bad, but they're not all the same. Some are just 'bad'; others are very, very bad and very dangerous. Poldy has become completely evil. He only shows me the evil side of his character. My bedroom is an evil place. It's evil in the daytime. It's evil when Poldy isn't there. It's evil all the time. What can I do? I don't know. I just don't know.

Until a month ago, I was all right during the day. I went to my study every day and wrote. This took my mind off Poldy. I thought of new adventures for Filbert Wiley and I enjoyed doing this. But during the past month I haven't been able to work. I still come to my study every day, but I sit at my desk and look out of the window. I don't write anything. I sleep very little. I eat very

little. I'm thin and weak. But today I'm writing. I'm writing these words. I'm writing quickly before it's too late. I have to write this story of my life with Poldy before it's too late.

You will ask: Why don't you tell Louis about this?

Louis still comes on Wednesdays and we still play chess. I never play chess well now and he always wins. I'm always tired and worried.

'What's the matter with you, William?' Louis asked last week. 'I can't understand. You're ill. You must see a doctor. I'm worried about you. If you don't call a doctor, *I'll* call one.'

Of course Louis mustn't call a doctor. 'Listen,' I said. 'I know I'm not very well. But I'll be better soon. I'm writing a very strange story about Filbert Wiley. I'll be better when I finish the story. I know I will. So please don't call a doctor. Do you promise?'

'All right, William,' Louis said. 'I promise.'

Louis is a good friend. I know he'll keep his promise.

Have I tried to tell Louis about Poldy? Yes, I have. Many times. But every time I try, I can't speak. I've tried to ask Louis to stay in the house with me for a night, but again, I can't. When I try to open my mouth, I can't. Then I always hear that 'knock, knock' from the room above. I always hear a message from Poldy. The words 'It's our secret' come into my head. Perhaps a real voice speaks these words. Perhaps it's Poldy's voice. It speaks kindly, but there's always a message in the voice.

One Wednesday about two months ago, I was playing chess with Louis. I was very tired after a very bad night. I tried to play chess and I didn't think of Poldy, but Louis suddenly remembered the name 'Poldy' and spoke to me during the game.

'William,' Louis said. 'I was in a bookshop the other day and I was looking at your books – the Filbert Wiley stories. I remember once – about five years ago – you spoke to me about a new character. You called this character "Poldy". I've never forgotten

34

his name because it's a strange name. I don't *like* the name, but I've always remembered it. I bought all your books from the last five years and took them home. I read them all and enjoyed them, but I didn't find this character "Poldy" in any of them.'

My face was white. Poldy was knocking hard on the floor of the room above. I could hear it, but Louis couldn't. In the end I said, 'Yes, Louis. I didn't use that character in my story. I changed the story.'

'Why?' Louis asked. 'I remember he was an interesting character, good and evil at the same time.'

'No!' I shouted. 'He's evil, evil, only evil!' The knock on the floor above was louder and louder. It was like a wild dance. I heard the message and stopped shouting. 'I'm sorry,' I said in a quiet voice. 'No, I didn't use that character.' (I couldn't say the name 'Poldy'.)

We continued to play chess. The game ended in the usual way. Louis said, 'You can't move anywhere,' and I lost. Louis said goodnight and left.

That night Poldy really punished me. He pushed me, kicked me and hit me. The funny thing is: you can never see any signs of this 'punishment' on my body. I'm often in great pain, but it never shows on my body. Then I made my fourth important discovery: Poldy didn't like Louis. He didn't want him to come to my house. He wanted to be alone with me all the time. The games on Tuesday nights (the nights before Louis came) were always very, very bad.

I don't enjoy Tuesday evenings now. I'm afraid of Tuesday nights. And it's Tuesday today!

Chapter 6   Monday Night

I want to tell you about last night in detail because we've never played a dangerous game like that before. I shake when I think of it. I'm shaking at this minute while I'm writing these words.

But I'll begin at the beginning. Yesterday I sat in my study all day. Of course, I didn't write a word. I didn't try to write anything. Filbert Wiley doesn't interest me. His adventures mean nothing to me.

So how did I spend the day? I looked out of the window all day. It's winter now, but it isn't very cold. Yesterday the sky was clear. The sun shone in a blue sky. I looked down at my garden. It was quiet and empty. The grass was wet. The trees were brown. Nothing happened all day. I saw only one sign of life: a fat black cat walked across the grass. It stood under my bedroom window and looked up at it for a long time. Then it went away very slowly. I remember that cat very well. I saw it once before. I heard it in my garden years ago – when my game with Poldy began to go wrong. The cat didn't worry me now. It wasn't important. My only worry was Poldy.

Perhaps you're thinking: there's no need to worry. You can go away for ever. You don't *have* to play games with a ghost. But I *want* to play. This game is part of my way of life. It's forever in my mind. So I must stay here to the end.

I know you want to hear about last night. But you must give me time. I need time to get everything in order. Very many things happened and I want to remember them all.

The sky stayed clear at night. There was a full moon. It was like a night that I've already described in this story. I was glad there was a full moon. My room was full of light. I didn't close my curtains before I went to bed. I had the moon for company. Perhaps it was midnight when I pulled the plug out. The game began immediately.

Poldy surprised me at the beginning of the game. He didn't begin with a bad game but a good one. I couldn't believe it! It was a very long time since our last good game. I was almost happy while we played. I didn't realize that this was a joke – an evil joke. At the beginning of the good game, Poldy gave a clear sign of his presence. I heard a knock at the other side of the room. Then he began to walk towards my bed while I tried to find the plug. He reached my bed. Then he shook it before I put the plug in. He won. So we began again. I usually want him to win the good games. But last night he really won. He was quicker than I was. This didn't worry me. But then something happened very suddenly and the good game stopped. My room suddenly became cold – very, very cold. I don't know why. My house is always warm. I began to shake. I hate the cold. It was at this minute that the good game stopped. I could suddenly feel evil in the air.

I wanted to be warm, so I covered my head with the bed clothes. I waited. A hand pulled the bed clothes off my bed very quickly. I sat up and watched. My bed clothes flew across the room and dropped onto the floor. I ran after them. But when I tried to reach them, they moved away from me. I think Poldy was saying, 'Catch me if you can.' I understood he wanted to play 'find me' with me.

'Very well,' I said loudly. 'We'll play "find me", but please give me my bed clothes.' The bed clothes flew onto my bed. 'Good,' I said. 'Now I'll count up to ten and you can hide.' I turned my head towards the wall and began to count: 'One, two, three . . .' I was counting very slowly. While I was counting, I heard footsteps behind me. I heard all kinds of little noises. Then the room was quiet. I turned round.

Of course, the room was empty. Poldy was hiding. But where was he? You can't hide in many places in my room. You can hide under the bed, under the chair and in the wardrobe. But Poldy is a ghost: he can hide anywhere. He can hide inside one of my pockets!

'I'm coming to find you, Poldy,' I said.

I went straight to the wardrobe. I opened the door very slowly. Before the door was wide open, I put my hand inside the wardrobe carefully. 'Perhaps Poldy will bite or hit me,' I thought. But he didn't. I pulled the door wide open. The moonlight shone into the wardrobe. I could see my clothes inside it. I could see my shirts, my trousers, my suits and my old coat. I could see Julie's beautiful dress. I touched all my clothes. Nothing. 'He's inside my coat,' I thought. I took the coat out of the wardrobe and shook it. Nothing again. 'Where are you?' I shouted. In wild fear, I took my clothes out one by one and shook them. Then I threw them onto the bedroom floor. Soon all my clothes were on the floor. Julie's party dress was on the floor too.

The wardrobe was empty, but Poldy gave no sign.

'You're under the bed!' I cried. I lay on the floor and went under the bed. I touched the floor with my hands – but there was nothing. I got up and walked round the room. I looked under the chair. Nothing. In the end, I sat on the chair and waited. He was in the room. I could feel that, but I couldn't find him.

I sat on the chair for a long time. I was sleepy and shut my eyes. When I opened them, I looked at my bed. This woke me up. The bed clothes were still there, but there was a shape under them. It was the shape of a person with bed clothes over his head. I went quietly towards the bed and touched the bed clothes. The 'person' moved under them. It moved like someone in his sleep. I touched them again. The shape threw the bed clothes back. I couldn't see anyone, but I heard quick footsteps to the other side of the room. Poldy's hiding place was under the bed clothes.

'I've caught you!' I cried. 'I've won! Now it's my turn to hide. You must count up to ten and I'll hide.'

I waited and then I heard a knock from the corner of the room. 'He's counting,' I thought. One knock, then another and another. 'Where can I hide?' I thought. There was only one place: under the bed. I went under it very quietly. Then I lay without moving. The knocks continued. There were ten of them, and then silence. I held my breath and listened. Complete silence. I looked across the floor. I could see the clothes that I threw there. Then the clothes began to move. Someone was picking them up and throwing them down again one by one. Shirts moved into the air and fell again. My trousers, my coat and my suits moved up and fell. Julie's dress shone in the moonlight: then it moved up and fell too. Poldy was carefully looking at all my clothes.

Suddenly, Poldy broke the silence. The wardrobe door flew open. He hit the wardrobe hard. The wardrobe shook. Then it fell and hit the floor with a loud noise. There was silence again. I stopped breathing. I heard the 'wooden leg' from the other side of the room. It came towards the bed very slowly. Knock, knock, knock, nearer and nearer and nearer. I wanted to scream. Poldy stopped next to my bed. I was very cold now and I pulled up my legs close to my body. Something touched my legs softly. I didn't move. Then something touched my face. I felt hot breath on my face and screamed loudly. I tried to move away, but couldn't. In my fear, I lay without moving. Then Poldy lifted the bed above my head and dropped it on top of me. It hit the floor loudly, but didn't touch me. Then he lifted it again. It almost touched the top of the room above me. I looked up at it in fear and it began to come down very slowly. In fear, I stood up and ran to the other side of the room. I looked at the bed. It returned to the floor softly. 'I must hide somewhere,' I thought. The wardrobe was on the floor in front of me. I turned it over. Then I climbed inside it and shut it. I lay there quietly.

Poldy began to knock at the wardrobe door, very quietly at first, then louder. Suddenly, the door flew open. A strong pair of hands took hold of me, picked me up and threw me onto the bed. I screamed and shouted, but I didn't feel any pain. I got under the bed clothes and waited.

For the first time I heard Poldy's 'voice'. I heard a long evil laugh. There was something in the voice that I knew. Soon the room was full of wild laughter.

'Stop it! Stop it! Please stop it!' I cried. The laughter continued for a long time and then stopped.

There was a very long silence after this. The game of 'find me' was at an end. 'What's he going to do next?' I thought. Perhaps half an hour passed and nothing happened.

Then I heard a strange noise. Someone was scratching. It was like fingers on glass. Was Poldy scratching the windows? I looked at them carefully and could see them clearly in the moonlight, but the sound didn't come from the windows. 'There isn't any more glass in the room', I thought. But I was wrong. There was the photo of Julie on the wall! The photo was behind glass. I listened. The scratching continued. The sound came from the picture. I looked at the picture carefully. It was a large photo of Julie's face. There she was, young and beautiful. She was smiling at me. In the moonlight, I couldn't see the details, of course. But I knew that photo so well! It was easy for me to imagine Julie's beautiful face. The scratching stopped and the photo moved off the wall and flew towards me slowly. Soon it was less than a metre away from me. I looked into Julie's eyes and she looked into mine. 'Is it you, Julie? Are you the ghost? Are you haunting me?' The answer to my questions was evil laughter. Julie always laughed softly, but I heard the sound of her voice in this evil laughter.

Chapter 7 The Truth

I've told you the truth in this story, but I haven't told you all the truth. Why? Because I haven't been able to tell the truth to myself, so how could I tell it to you? I haven't faced the truth for twelve years now. But the time has come to tell it. Perhaps you already know. Yes, I killed Julie. But please believe me. I killed her out of love, not hate.

Julie loved me and I loved her. I've told you that and it's true. Julie and I were happy. That's true, too. My friends were jealous of me. That's also true. But I haven't told you one thing: I was jealous of my friends.

You know a lot about me now. You know I'm not an interesting person. I don't go out much. I don't dance. I haven't got many friends. My life is in my books. In our twelve years together, Julie changed my life. She filled my life with friends and with laughter. So why did I kill her?

We went out together a lot. Friends often came to our house. Julie liked company. She liked my company, but she liked other people's company too. But I wanted Julie for myself and only for myself. At parties I was always alone. There were always young men round Julie. They were always dancing with her. She enjoyed their company. Of course, Julie was my wife and I was her husband. But that wasn't enough for me. I didn't want Julie to speak to other men. I didn't want her to dance with other men. I wanted her to be with *me* all the time. When I saw other men round her, I was always jealous. I couldn't hide my jealousy. One day I spoke to her about it. I can't remember our words exactly, but they were something like this:

'Put your suit on, William. We're going out tonight.'

'I don't want to go out,' I answered.

'Don't be silly, William. We're going *out*.'

'But I want to stay here,' I said.

'You always want to stay at home,' Julie said. 'I know you want to write your books. But we must live too.'

'But I don't like to be with so many people,' I said. 'I only want to be with you.'

'William!' Julie said kindly. 'You're jealous.'

I had to agree. 'I know I am,' I said.

'There's no need to be jealous,' she said. 'I love you and you know it.'

'Yes, I know it very well.'

'Your character is different from mine. I need a lot of people round me,' Julie said. 'I can't be in this house all the time – alone with you.'

'I'm afraid I'll lose you,' I said.

'You must never fear that,' Julie said. 'You'll never lose me. I love you and I'm your wife.'

'I want you to be my wife forever,' I said.

'And I will be,' Julie answered.

She was telling the truth, but I was still very jealous. In time, I got more and more jealous. I couldn't hide it.

Then something happened. I've already told you about it. Julie became ill. She was very, very ill. I called the best doctors. I've told you that and it's true. 'Your wife is very ill,' one of them said to me. 'She has a weak heart. She must be careful. People with weak hearts sometimes die very suddenly.'

I was afraid to lose Julie. I wanted her to live. But I wanted her to be mine forever. Then an evil idea came into my mind. I thought: 'I can kill Julie and she'll be mine. After that, I'll never go

out and she'll always be with me.' I thought about this idea a lot. I knew I had to kill her. That's why I've never looked for another wife since Julie. She's with me all the time: I have her pictures and I have my memories of her. I'm not jealous now because I don't need to be jealous.

One night she lay next to me. She was very ill and was breathing softly. She was awake and I spoke to her.

'Julie,' I said softly. 'I want you to be mine forever. You love me and I love you. That's the secret of our happiness.'

'Yes, that's our secret,' she answered softly.

'You'll always stay with me in this house,' I said.

'Yes,' she answered.

Then, very softly, I put my pillow over her face and held it there. I held it there for a long time. She tried to move away, but she couldn't. She was very weak. I could hear her cries, but I didn't take the pillow away. At last, her heart stopped. She was dead.

'That's our secret,' I said, when she died. 'Now you're mine forever.'

I phoned the doctor immediately. 'Julie isn't breathing very well,' I told him. The doctor arrived quickly, but of course, Julie was dead.

'I'm sorry to say this, Mr Harris,' he said, 'but your wife is dead. Her heart's stopped. She died a short time ago. Perhaps she died in her sleep.'

I cried a lot, but in my heart I was glad. I was glad because Julie was mine forever.

Today it's Tuesday, January 25th. I killed my dearest Julie twelve years ago today, on January 25th, 1988.

Chapter 8   Monday Night Continued

I moved away from my story because I wanted to tell you the truth. You think I'm crazy. Perhaps I *am* out of my mind. I've lived with this secret for twelve years now: I'm a murderer. I murdered my wife. My house has been haunted since then.

And last night I realized the truth for the first time in twelve years.

The ghost in my bedroom isn't a playful poltergeist. Its name isn't 'Poldy'. It's the ghost of my dear wife, Julie. It was a playful ghost at first. But now it's jealous and evil – as I was twelve years ago.

Last night I suddenly saw Julie 'alive' again. Her 'head' was the photo; her 'body' was the dress. She was dancing round the room. Oh, she danced very beautifully! Her beautiful dress was shining in the moonlight. I sat in bed and watched her. I forgot about the evil laughter. I forgot about my fears and worries. I forgot about our game. I could only think of Julie – 'alive' again after all these years. 'It's not possible,' I said to myself. 'I can't believe it.' Julie continued to dance and dance. I could hear music in my mind. I suddenly saw myself at a party. There was noise and laughter in the room. There were young men all round the room. My Julie was dancing to the music and the young men were looking at her. Then they looked at me and laughed. While they were laughing at me, I became angry and jealous. My mind became full of evil. 'Go away!' I screamed at the young men. 'Julie is mine, mine! Can't you see?' The young men laughed louder and louder.

I became angrier and angrier. I jumped out of bed and ran towards the dancing ghost. The music continued to play in my mind. The young men continued to watch me and to laugh at me. I picked up a chair and hit the young men with it. Then I hit the dancing ghost. I hit the beautiful dress while it was moving round the room. Suddenly, the music in my mind stopped. The dancing stopped. The young men in the room disappeared. Their faces became shadows – then nothing. Their laughter stopped.

I hit the dress again, not the picture, but just the dress. It shook, then it fell slowly to the floor. The photo was still at the top of the dress. The photo and the dress lay on the floor. Julie's smiling eyes looked up at me from the floor. 'They've gone,' I said softly. 'The young men have gone. You're mine again. All mine.'

I stood next to the dress and looked at it for a long time. Nothing happened: it didn't move. I touched it. It was real. I touched the photo. It was real too. Julie's eyes smiled at me from behind the glass. 'I want you to be mine forever,' I said to the photo, and I went back to my bed and got a pillow. Then I returned to the dress on the floor. I put the pillow over the photo and held it there. I held it there for a long time. The dress tried to move away but couldn't. Soft cries came from the photo. In the end, the dress stopped moving. I smiled to myself. 'I've murdered Julie a second time,' I thought. I laughed loudly.

Suddenly, a great scream came from the photo on the floor. One scream, then another and another. I jumped back in fear. The screaming stopped. The photo of Julie began to change. It wasn't smiling now. It was crying. I touched the glass on the photo. It was wet. Then the photo moved away from my hand. I stood up. The photo began to move off the floor very, very slowly. It came towards me and stopped in front of my face. Then it fell to the floor and the glass broke into a thousand pieces. A 'hand' began to pull the photo into little pieces. It pulled off the hair, the eyes, the nose, the mouth. Soon there were little pieces of paper on the floor next to the dress. Then a great wind went through the room. It threw the dress across the floor. It threw the little pieces of paper to every part of the room. They fell to the floor slowly, like snow. Then the wind stopped.

The ghost was still in the room. I could feel it. 'That's the end of the game,' I thought. 'I'll go back to bed and put the plug in. I've had enough of this.' I picked up the pillow from the floor and went back to bed.

I was very tired and wanted to sleep. I reached over the side of the bed to find the plug. 'I'll send the ghost away and go to sleep,' I thought. I touched the plug. But when I touched it, I heard evil laughter. Then I realized the game wasn't finished!

The plug moved away from my hand. I tried to find it again. Every time I touched it, it moved away. I took hold of the cord and 'followed' it with my fingers. Then I found the plug again but couldn't pick it up. It moved across the floor. I got out of bed. I was on my knees on the floor. I could see the plug in the moonlight. I could see it very clearly. I went towards it on my knees. When I reached it, it moved away again. The evil laughter continued. 'Please, Julie,' I said. 'Please give me the plug.' The plug came towards me and danced in front of my eyes, but I couldn't touch it. 'I'm not going to play now,' I said. 'I'm leaving the room.' I got up and went towards the door.

I tried to open the door but couldn't. I hit the door hard with my hands. I pushed and pulled, but I couldn't open it! I was a prisoner in my own room. 'Where can I go? What can I do?' I cried. 'I'm your prisoner now. I must get out. Please let me out. Please! Please!'

The evil laughter stopped. The room was silent. Then something hit the window lightly. After this, I heard a scratching sound – like fingers on glass. 'It isn't the glass over Julie's photo,' I thought. I listened again. The sound was coming from the window. I went towards it and looked out. There was a face at the window – not Julie's face or the face of any person. It was the face of a cat! The cat was looking into my room. It wasn't the fat black cat. It was a white cat. 'I've seen this cat before somewhere,' I thought, 'but where?' I tried to think. Suddenly, I remembered. Of course! It was Julie's cat. Julie loved animals. She had a cat like this when she was alive: a beautiful white cat.

When Julie died – I mean, after I murdered her – the cat disappeared. I never saw it again. But now it was back. I looked through the window. The cat's face was against mine. Only the glass was between us. The cat's eyes were red and angry. It scratched the glass wildly. I hit the glass from the inside, but the cat didn't go away. It began to cry like a baby. 'Stop it! Stop it!' I screamed.

I ran back to the bedroom door and tried to open it. Again, it wasn't possible. The cat continued to cry outside the window. I suddenly wanted to kill it. I looked round the room and tried to find something. I was really angry. My wardrobe was still on the floor. There were broken pieces everywhere. I picked up a thick piece of wood and ran towards the window.

The cat looked at me with its red eyes. It cried louder and louder. I hit the window hard with the piece of wood. It broke into a thousand pieces. I laughed. Then I looked through the broken window, but there was nothing there. No cat, no sound, nothing! 'Wonderful,' I thought. 'It's gone away. Perhaps it was never there. Perhaps I only imagined it. I must stay calm. I'm imagining things.'

But I wasn't imagining things. I heard a sound behind me and jumped. It was the sound of a baby. I turned round in fear and there it was! The white cat! It was looking up at me and there was blood on its face! I looked at my hands. There was blood on them, too! I was still holding the piece of wood. 'So you're still alive!' I screamed at the cat. I ran towards it and tried to hit it again. I hit the floor hard. I hit the cat over the head. I tried to hit it again, but it wasn't there. Then it appeared again in another corner of the room. It was looking at me with its red eyes. I ran after it and tried to hit it. Every time I tried to do this, the cat disappeared. Every time it appeared, it was red with blood. Soon its body was red with blood, but it appeared again and again. Here! There! In front of me! Behind me! On the floor! On the bed! In the air! At last, the crying stopped. The cat disappeared and didn't come back.

'All these things have happened in my mind', I thought. 'It was my imagination, just my imagination. I must keep calm. Now, what was I doing? Yes. The plug. I was looking for the plug. I must find it. I'm a prisoner in my own room. The ghost is playing jokes on me. If I find the plug, I can send it away.'

I got down on my knees to look for the plug. It was still on the floor next to my bed. I went towards it slowly and quietly like a cat. The plug was a bird and I was a cat. 'I'm going to catch you, little bird,' I said softly. Nearer and nearer. Then I jumped! The plug was in my hands. I had it! I had it! 'Now I must find the socket.' I touched the wall with my fingers. The socket. 'Yes. Here it is.' The ghost didn't pull the plug out of my hands. I put the plug into the socket and the light came on.

I got into bed and lay back. At last! My room was full of light. I looked round the room and couldn't believe my eyes. There wasn't any broken glass on the floor. The wardrobe wasn't on the floor. The window wasn't broken. All the things in my room were in order. The photo of Julie was on the wall. Julie's face was smiling down at me. The wardrobe was in its place in the corner of the room. The wardrobe door was shut. I got up and opened it. My clothes were in the wardrobe. Julie's dress was there too. My chair was in its place. I went to the bedroom door and tried to open it. It opened easily. I shut it again.

Then I began to laugh at myself. 'I imagined all these things,' I said. 'The dance, the cat – they were just my imagination.' I went

back to bed. I looked at my bedside clock. It was 3.30. I sat in bed for about ten minutes. I was thinking. The light was on, but I could feel something strange. The ghost was still in the room. The plug was back in place, but the ghost was still there! 'It's broken the last rule of the game,' I thought. 'I've put the plug in, but it hasn't gone away!'

This thought filled me with fear! All the rules were broken now. The ghost didn't disappear when the light came on. I switched the light off (from the switch), but the 'evil presence' was still there. I pulled the plug out and put it back a number of times, but the ghost stayed in the room. The room was in order but full of evil.

I switched off the light and tried to sleep, but I couldn't. Then I tried to sleep with the light on, but I couldn't. In the end, I turned the light off and lay in bed. The moon was still shining brightly. The ghost didn't play any jokes now; it stayed in my room quietly. It was 'there' all the time. I lay in bed and listened, but the room was silent. I could hear my heart. I could hear my own breathing.

I lay in bed for a long time. My eyes were open. I could see every detail of my room in the moonlight. Suddenly, I heard heavy breathing. It was coming from a corner of the room. Then I saw a dark shadow in the corner of the room. It was like a black cloud. The sound of heavy breathing was coming from the shadow. The shadow began to move towards me very slowly. I tried to jump out of bed, but couldn't move in my fear. I lay there and the thin black cloud came nearer and nearer and nearer. Soon it was high in the air above my bed. I looked up at it. Then it began to come down on me. The room was now in complete darkness. The shadow cut out the moonlight. Soon it was over me and all round me. I could still hear heavy breathing. I could feel hot breath on my face: the breath of an evil ghost. I tried to scream, but couldn't. I had no breath.

At the same time I could hear another sound. It came from outside. It was the sound of a cat outside my window. The cat was crying like a baby.

I lay under the dark shadow. I knew it was the shadow of death.

Chapter 9   Today is Tuesday

Last night I was in the shadow of death, but I'm still alive. At this minute I'm in my study and I'm writing this story. It's only 10.00 p.m. but I'm very tired. I didn't sleep for a minute last night.

The shadow didn't hurt me. When the morning light came, the shadow disappeared. I got up and left my bedroom. The shadow disappeared, but the ghost was still in the room. In fact, it's still there now.

I'm in my study now and the ghost can't hurt me here (I hope!). I came to my study at 5.30 this morning. I've written this story since that time. My desk is covered with papers. I've been here for more than sixteen hours and I'm still writing. I haven't eaten. I haven't washed and I'm still wearing my night clothes. It's cold outside. My night clothes are made of thin cloth – but I can't feel the cold. I can only feel one thing: I'm very, very tired.

I'm near the end of my story. In one long day I've tried to describe my life since Julie's death. Perhaps you don't believe that any of these things happened. Perhaps you think I'm crazy. Perhaps you're saying: You're a murderer and your mind has punished you. Perhaps you think there was no ghost. It was all in my mind: I made it all up. If you think any of these things, you're wrong. All these things really happened.

My story began with a playful poltergeist and ended with an evil ghost. At the beginning we played a happy game. But in time this game became a dangerous one. This game has continued for twelve years and Julie was my wife for twelve years. The game is

like my life with Julie. At the beginning I was happy with her, but I became jealous of her friends. Then my mind became evil and I murdered Julie and murdered our life together. I wanted Julie to be mine and only mine. The same thing happened in the game. At the beginning it was a happy one. Then the ghost became jealous. It wanted me to be alone. It became evil and has tried to kill me.

Now there's only one question on my mind: will the ghost murder me?

Just now, I'm trying not to think about this question. I'll find out the answer when I go to bed. I don't want to think about it now.

But what can I think about? Nothing in my past is important to me now. Filbert Wiley's adventures are like a dream. The game with the ghost has become my life. But I can stop the game and change my life. There's one way I can do it. I must tell this secret to someone. Then I know the game will stop. Tomorrow Louis will be here, but I won't play chess with him. I'll tell him this story. Then I'll be all right again. What will Louis think when I tell him the story? I don't know. The game will end if I tell Louis the secret. But that's a big 'if'. Will I tell Louis my secret? I don't know. If I live through the night, then I'll tell him. If I don't live, then my story will be in these papers. Perhaps Louis will find these papers and publish them. But they aren't in order! There are papers all over my desk. There aren't any numbers on the pages. I've written everything in pencil and it's hard to read. If Louis wants to publish these papers, he'll have to put them in order and type them again. I think he can sort them out very well. I haven't thought of a good title for the book. Perhaps *Dangerous Game* is a good title. But my fears are making me crazy. I'm not going to die. *I'll* put the papers in order and publish the book. Louis will never see these papers.

It's been a strange day: strange in many ways. I haven't written a word for a month, but today I've written a book. It's January 25th – twelve years' exactly since Julie's death. We've been together for twenty-four years. What a day it's been! Yesterday the sun shone in a clear sky. But today it's been dark and cloudy – a real winter's day. I'll remember today for a long time.

During the day, while writing, I've looked out of the window a few times. Now it's dark, of course. But earlier my garden was empty – no cats or anything like that. But I haven't had time to look out of the window very much. My story has been on my mind all day. I've tried to remember every detail. I've tried to tell you every detail.

Try to imagine me at this minute. I'm sitting at my desk. My desk light is on. I haven't closed the curtains of my study. The moon is up and I can see it through my study window. I'm alone in this big house. The house is dark and silent. My bedroom is at the other end of the house and sooner or later I must go to it. The bedroom door is shut, but someone is behind it. I know Julie's ghost is in the room. I know the ghost is waiting for me. I'll go into an evil world when I go into that room. When you're afraid, you look behind you all the time. You don't like the dark. Remember when you were a child? My bed was against the wall when I was a child. I never slept with my face towards the wall. I was afraid there was 'something' behind me. I still have this fear. Tonight I have to go into my bedroom alone, and perhaps I'll never come out of it again alive.

I've always been afraid of ghosts. When, as a child, I closed my curtains, I always looked at them. There were flowers on my curtain cloth, but I always saw faces in those flowers. Sometimes they were happy faces, sometimes they were evil faces. When I turned off the light, I often imagined those faces in the room all round me. Sometimes I cried and my mother came into the room. But if I cry tonight, who will come into my room? Who will say, 'It's all right, my dearest. Go to sleep now. You've had a bad dream.'? Nobody. I'll be alone. Alone with Poldy – Julie – the ghost.

You'll ask: Why don't you leave the house? There's still time. Don't stay here. Don't play the game tonight. But I *must* play the game once more. I'm very sleepy, but I'll wake up. I always wake up when the game begins.

Why don't I phone Louis? He can come here and stay with me tonight. I'll tell you something. I've tried to phone Louis a number of times this evening, but my line is dead. I hear nothing when I pick up the phone. I'm cut off from the world.

So there's only one thing that I can do. I must play the game. What kind of game will it be tonight? I shake when I think about it. My heart is full of fear. My hand is shaking now while I'm writing these words. What will happen? I'll go into the bedroom. I won't have to pull out the plug to bring the ghost. The ghost is there already. I'll go to bed and the game will begin. But what kind of game will it be? How will it end?

I know I'm talking too much – writing too much. I haven't got any more to tell you. So why am I writing? Because I want you to be with me. I'm writing because I'm afraid to leave this study. I'm all right here. But when I stop, I'll have to go to my bedroom. I think that time has come now. I must stop now. So I'll say 'goodnight' to you – or perhaps it's 'goodbye'. Perhaps it's goodbye – forever.

Chapter 10   The End

My name is Louis. I was William Harris's friend – as you already know from his story. I've added this ending to his book to complete the story. William died on the night of January 25th, 2000. I talked to the police doctor. William died just before midnight: about an hour after he went to bed.

Why did William die? Nobody can explain that. It's a mystery like so many things in his story. His life was a mystery and his death was a mystery too. William had no family and I was his only friend. The police have asked me many questions about William. But I haven't been able to tell them more than what is in his book. A lot of police officers have read William's papers. Some of them believe his story, others don't believe it. His death is a mystery.

I found the pages of *Dangerous Game* in William's study on the night after his death. A few days later, I was able to take the papers home. All the papers were in the study, exactly as William left them. There were papers all over the desk and all over the floor. There were a lot of pencils on the desk too.

I'm writing this ending to William's story six months after his death. I've just finished my work on his papers. William wrote *Dangerous Game* (I think the title is a good one) in one long day. But I needed six months to read and type his work. There weren't any numbers on the pages, so it took a long time to put them in order. William wrote the book very quickly and the pages were very hard to read. He didn't write in complete sentences. So it was very hard for me to turn the papers into a real book. I've broken the work into chapters. I hope it's been easy to read. I've given each chapter a title, but I haven't added a word to William's story and I haven't cut out anything. It's just as he wrote it. I've published this story because William wanted me to publish it.

During this time I've asked myself many questions about William. Some of the answers to my questions are in William's book, but many aren't.

For example, I knew William wasn't well – in his mind, I mean. There was always something on his mind. I could see this every time we met. He didn't eat well and he didn't sleep well. I could see this too. During the year before his death, he became thinner and thinner. He wasn't interested in food, in his work, in the chess games that we played. In fact, he wasn't interested in life. I'm sure he was interested in something. But this 'something' was a mystery to me. He never told me about it. It was his secret. I wanted to call a doctor, but he never let me. During the year before his death, our games of chess were becoming silly. William never played seriously. He often stopped during a game and looked up towards the room above. He was trying to hear something. I once asked him about 'Poldy' and he didn't want to tell me anything. Do you remember? In his book he says there was a knocking sound from the room above. Was there *really* a knocking sound? I don't know. I never heard anything.

Was William crazy? Did all these things *really* happen, or did he imagine them? I don't know. I'm sure William had a wonderful imagination. Perhaps you've read his Filbert Wiley stories. If you *have* read them, you'll know a lot about William's imagination. In one of these stories (I can't remember the title) Filbert Wiley is a prisoner in a haunted house. Perhaps you remember the story. I thought of it when I read this book. William was a real writer. In his story William often says he was an 'uninteresting person'. It's true he didn't have an interesting life. (And what does interesting really mean?) But I'm sure he had an interesting mind. You can see his mind at work in his detective stories. You can see it at work in this book.

Did William murder Julie? Another interesting question! It isn't possible to say. I'm sure he loved her deeply.

Perhaps William *was* jealous, but he never showed it. He described Julie very well in his story. She was a wonderful person. We all loved her. Of course, she was very different in character from William. People enjoyed being with her. She was always laughing and singing. She was very good company. She helped William a lot. She showed him the world. He enjoyed his life with Julie. After her death, he became a different person. He cut himself off from the world. He did nothing except work. In the end, I was his only friend. That's because I knew him from our student days. I knew him before he met Julie. I knew him very well. But there's still a lot that I don't know about him. Did he murder Julie? I find this hard to believe. But perhaps he *did* murder her. One strange fact is true. William died on the date that Julie died: January 25th, twelve years after her death. I can't explain it.

I knew William wasn't well. I often asked him to leave his house. I asked him to come and stay with me, but he didn't want to leave his own place. Once or twice I offered to stay with him, but he didn't want my company. So after our chess games on a Wednesday, I always went home. We never talked very much during our games. I know he enjoyed my company. I enjoyed his. In his story he says he tried to phone me on the night of his death. He says the line was dead. That's a mystery too. I used the phone after I found him. I called the police, and the phone was in order. Did William imagine it was out of order? Was it really out of order? If it was, how did this happen?

So either William's story is true or it isn't. If it *is* true, then we must accept it. William was haunted by an evil, jealous ghost.

(Whose ghost? I can't say.) Perhaps the story isn't true. Then we must believe that William imagined it all. This means that he was haunted by his own imagination. In the end, he really went crazy: he didn't live in our world. His imagination killed him. This can happen, of course, but we will never know the answer to the mystery.

Now I can only describe in detail the night of Wednesday, January 26th, 2000.

I arrived at William's house at my usual time: just before eight o'clock. The house was completely dark and this surprised me. There was usually a light on somewhere. I knocked at the front door and waited. There was no reply. This surprised me too. William usually opened the door immediately. 'Perhaps he's gone out,' I thought. 'But no, that's not possible. He doesn't often go out and he's always at home on a Wednesday. He's never been out on a Wednesday.'

I knocked at the door more loudly, but there was still no reply. I tried to open the front door, but I couldn't. So I went to the back door. I knocked at this too and waited. Again, there was no reply. I tried to open this door too, but couldn't. I called out 'William!' very loudly a number of times. There was no answer. I threw a few small stones lightly at the windows upstairs. Nobody came to any of the windows. 'This is very strange,' I thought. I went round the house and looked at all the windows on the ground floor. They were shut. But in the end, I found a small window that was open. It was the kitchen window at the back of the house. I climbed through it (and it wasn't easy!) and turned on the kitchen light.

The kitchen was in order. William lived alone, but he was a very tidy person. The room was clean and tidy. I went straight to the living room. We always played chess in this room. I turned on the light. Again, the room was in order. The chess board was on the table. The chess pieces were in a wooden box next to the board. 'That's strange,' I thought. 'William usually puts the pieces on the board before I arrive.' He's always ready for a game.

When I noticed this, I began to worry. I began to call out William's name louder and louder. The name 'William' rang through the empty house, but there was no reply. I went out of the living room and stood at the foot of the stairs. I called up the stairs: 'William!' Nobody answered me.

Suddenly, worry became fear – fear for William! What was the matter? I ran upstairs, three steps at a time, and went straight to the study. 'Perhaps he's still working and hasn't heard me,' I thought. I knocked at the study door and waited. There was no light under the door. Nobody answered, so I went in. I switched on the light. The room was very untidy. There were papers on the desk and on the floor. I didn't look at the papers at the time. It wasn't my business. I write books myself and I don't like other people to read my papers! I didn't know then that those papers were the pages of this book. They were the pages of the book that I've just finished working on. I discovered this later – when the police came. The police read William's story first and after a few days they gave it to me.

When I left William's study, I didn't go straight to his bedroom for a very simple reason. Don't forget, it was only just after eight o'clock. It was too early for anyone to be in bed. I went to every other room in the house. I was calling his name all the time. In the end, there was only one more room, the bedroom, and I went to it.

The bedroom door was shut. I knocked at the door gently and waited. I knocked again. Nothing. I opened the door very gently: the room was quite dark. It was very cold in the room, I remember – but other parts of the house were warm. I began to shake in William's room. I don't know why, but I felt a strange fear. Was someone in the room? Was someone watching? (Perhaps I only imagined this!) I touched the wall to find the light switch.

But in my fear (my heart was going wildly), I couldn't find it.

Then I kicked something. I touched it: it was William's bedside table. I touched the top of the table and found the bedside light. I pressed the switch but the light didn't come on. Then I kicked something on the floor: it was the plug. I got down on my knees and found it. 'Why isn't it in the socket?' I thought.

I put the plug into the socket and the light came on. When I stood up, I looked round the room. I couldn't believe my eyes! It was very untidy and in a terrible state. Two windows were broken and there was glass on the floor. There were clothes on the floor, too – William's clothes and one of Julie's party dresses. The wardrobe was completely broken and there were pieces of wood on the floor. There were small pieces of paper, too. I picked up one or two pieces. I realized they were part of a photograph. A cold wind came through the broken windows. I could hear a cat out in the cold. It was crying like a baby, poor thing!

I wanted to run out of the room, but I had to find William first. The double bed was against the wall. There was a shape under the bed clothes. There was a pillow at the top end of the bed. It was over the head of the person in the bed. I picked the pillow up very gently. It was right over William's face. I knew immediately that he was dead. The face filled me with fear. The eyes were wide open and the mouth was wide open, too. There were signs of fear in William's face. The eyes looked up at me: they looked up in fear.

I put the pillow back over William's face very gently. I didn't want to touch anything before the police arrived. I stood in front of the body for a long time. I was too afraid to move. The room was evil, so evil!

While I stood there, I noticed something strange on the pillow. There was a clear shape on it – like the shape of a hand.

ACTIVITIES

Chapters 1–3

Before you read

1 This book is called *Dangerous Game*. How many dangerous games can you think of? Do you play any of them?

2 Find these words in your dictionary. They are all in the story. Make a sentence with both words in it.

   a *appear, character*

   b *board, chess*

   c *cord, evil*

   d *ghost, haunt*

   e *jealous, poltergeist*

   f *plug, socket*

3 If you are interested in the *details* of a story, are you interested in:

   a everything about it?

   b nothing about it?

After you read

4 Are these sentences true or untrue? Correct the statements that are not true.

   a William Harris is best known as a writer of ghost stories.

   b William and Julie were very different.

   c Louis is a character in William's book.

   d Poldy disappears when William turns off the bedside light with the switch.

5 Discuss these questions.

   a Louis says, 'You've really lost the game now.' What does he mean? What is William thinking about?

   b The writer says, 'Poldy and laughter go together – I mean they went together at first.' What does he mean? How are William's feelings for Poldy changing?

Chapters 4–6

Before you read

6 What are the rules of the games with Poldy? What do you think is going to happen in future games?

7 Answer these questions. Find the words in *italics* in your dictionary.

   a Describe these things. What are they for?

      curtain   wardrobe

   b Show the class how you do these.

      – take a deep *breath* (*breathe* deeply)

      – *scratch* your arm

After you read

8 What happens when:

   a the wardrobe door opens?

   b William tries to close the curtains?

   c he tries to sleep in his study?

   d he turns off the light with the switch?

   e he thinks about telling Louis?

9 Which is the worst game, do you think? Why? Describe the game to other students.

Chapters 7–10

Before you read

10 Discuss possible endings to the story. How do you think it will end?

11 Find these words in your dictionary. Use them in the questions below. Discuss answers to the questions.

    pillow   publish   truth

    a Is William telling us the .... about his life?

    b Has William .... his story?

    c Why is a .... important to the story?

After you read

12 What really happened to William's wife? Why? What do other people believe about her death?

13 Work with another student. Act out this conversation.

　　Student A:　You are Louis. A police officer has just arrived at William's house. Tell him/her what you found. Answer the police officer's questions.

　　Student B:　You are the police officer. Ask Louis what he knows about William's death. Ask about his health, his life and his feelings.

Writing

14 Write about William's life and death for a writers' magazine.

15 William says that he is not an interesting person. Do you agree? Why (not)?

16 Write a letter from Louis to a friend about William's death and Louis' feelings about him and his story.

17 Does *Dangerous Game* sound like a true story? Why (not)?

Answers for the Activities in this book are available from your local office or alternatively write to: Penguin Readers Marketing Department, Pearson Education, Edinburgh Gate, Harlow, Essex CM20 2JE.